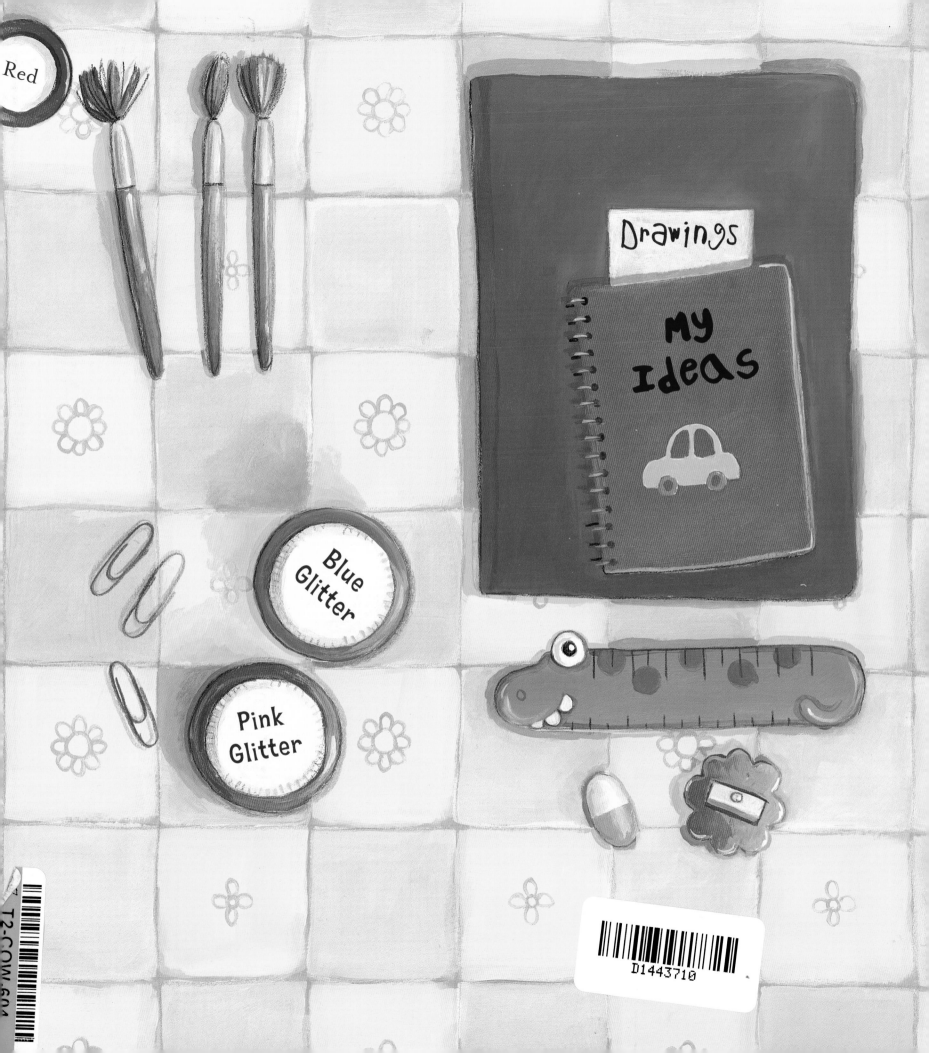

For Charlotte, with all my love xx ~ T. C.

For my cousin Felicity ~ A. E.

Copyright © 2012 by Good Books, Intercourse, PA 17534
International Standard Book Number: 978-1-56148-746-2
Library of Congress Catalog Card Number: 2011031771

Text copyright © Tracey Corderoy 2012
Illustrations copyright © Alison Edgson 2012
Original edition published in English by Little Tiger Press,
an imprint of Magi Publications, London, England, 2012
LTP/1800/0292/1011 • Printed in China

Library of Congress Cataloging-in-Publication Data

Corderoy, Tracey.
Just one more! / Tracey Corderoy ; [illustrated by] Alison Edgson.
p. cm.
Summary: Little Brown Bunny always wants just one more book
read to him at bedtime, so he spends all day creating a bedtime
book that is so long the story will last all night.
ISBN 978-1-56148-746-2 (hardcover : alk. paper)
[1. Books and reading--Fiction. 2. Bedtime--Fiction. 3. Rabbits--Fiction.]
I. Edgson, Alison, ill. II. Title.
PZ7.C815354Ju 2012
[E]--dc23
2011031771

Just One More!

Tracey Corderoy   Alison Edgson

Good Books

Intercourse, PA 17534, 800/762-7171
www.GoodBooks.com

Snacktime was over. Bathtime was over.
That meant just one thing . . .
　　"Storytime!" cried Little Brown Bunny.
　　So Mommy read him a story.
Then another. Then *another*!

"Just *one* more," begged Bunny.

So Daddy read him one more story, right to the end.

Still Bunny said, "Just one more?"

"Grandma's turn!" sighed Daddy Rabbit.

When Grandma had read *all* the dragon books,

and Grandpa had read them *again*, Bunny still wanted . . .
"Just one more!"

Mommy yawned a great big yawn.
"We've read all your stories!
And no more stories means it's
time to sleep," she said.
"Oh," said Bunny.

"Maybe," he whispered,
"I'll *make* a bedtime book.
A super-long one! Then
storytime will last *all night*."

Next morning Little Brown Bunny hopped
out of bed.

"Hooray!" he cried. "Time to make
my story!"

He bounced across to his making-things box.
Soon he was writing big, long words and
drawing lots of pictures.

At last, he heaved up his heavy book.
This was going to be the longest
story *ever*!

"Are you sitting comfortably?"
he asked his toys. "We might be here
a long, long time!"

Two minutes later, it was all over.
"MO-O-OM!" called Bunny.
"My super-long story wasn't
super-long at all."

"Don't worry," said Mom. "Why don't you ask your friends what stories *they* like? Then you can add them to your book."

"Great idea!" cried Bunny, and off he went.

CARROT COTTAGE

Little Owl was playing with his rocket when Bunny bounced in.

"*My* favorite stories," he hooted, "are ones about flying to the mooooooon! **Zooooom!**"

"I love the moon, too!" said Little Brown Bunny.
"Thanks, Owl!"
    And he blasted off to find Little Mouse . . .

Little Mouse was having a teeny snack when Bunny bounded in. "I love stories about cheese," she mumbled. "Big cheese, small cheese, round cheese, square cheese— *any* cheese really!"

"Thanks, Mouse," giggled Bunny, holding his nose. And off he raced to find Little Wolf . . .

Little Wolf was having a tea party when Bunny came by.

"Well, I do love stories about piggies!" he said. "And about Grandma with the big, furry ears!"

"*My* favorite story," grinned Big Daddy Wolf, "is the one about . . ."

"Hugs!"

"Oh, Daddy," giggled Little Wolf, "what big *arms* you have!"

"All the better to hug you with!" chuckled Daddy Wolf. And he gave Little Wolf a kiss on the nose.

"Thanks for your help," called
Bunny. And he hopped all the
way home!

Little Brown Bunny got out his book and scribbled down stories of moons made of cheese and rockets and big hugs.

By the time he had finished, it was dark outside.

"Come on, everyone!" he called. "This is going to be the best, most super-duper storybook *ever!*"

He opened his book ever so
carefully and took a big,
deep breath. Then Little
Brown Bunny . . .

. . . fell fast asleep!